NOW YOU SEE IT!

By Simcha Whitehill

SCHOLASTIC INC.

ISBN 978-0-545-89237-7

10 9 8 7 6 5 4 3 2 1   16 17 18 19 20

Printed in Malaysia   106

First printing 2016

POKÉMON EVOLUTION IN ACTION!

Want to see some of your favorite Pokémon evolve? Just place your thumb on the outside of this book and start flipping!

 If you put your thumb on the top, you'll see each Pokémon in its pre-evolved form.

 If you put your thumb in the middle, you'll see each Pokémon's first Evolution.

 If you put your thumb on the bottom, you'll see each Pokémon in its second evolved form—or its Mega-Evolved form!

Are you ready?

Now you see it . . . Now you don't!

CHESPIN

The Spiny Nut Pokémon

Height: 1' 04"
Weight: 19.8 lbs.
Type: Grass

CHESPIN

QUILLADIN

CHESNAUGHT

Chespin is one hardheaded Pokémon, but it's got a point—actually, it's got five of them! This Grass-type Pokémon's protective shell-like helmet is covered in soft spikes. When the Spiny Nut Pokémon is ready to battle, it flexes the five points and turns them into spears sharp enough to pierce stone. With that kind of prickly power, it's no wonder Chespin is a popular First Partner for Trainers in Kalos!

Sometimes a Trainer doesn't pick a First Partner, it picks them. That was the case with Ash's buddy Clemont and his Chespin. When Team Rocket kidnapped Professor Sycamore, Chespin helped Ash and Clemont find him. Then Chespin asked Clemont to join him on his journey. The two have been together ever since.

QUILLADIN
The Spiny Armor Pokémon

Height: 2' 04"
Weight: 63.9 lbs.
Type: Grass

CHESPIN

QUILLADIN

CHESNAUGHT

When Chespin evolves into Quilladin, it experiences quite a growth spurt! Quilladin is double the height and triple the weight of its pre-evolved form.

This roly-poly Grass-type Pokémon might seem so cute you want to hug it, but beware: It's not a Pokémon you should squeeze. Those quills on its back are actually sharp points. Plus, Quilladin's bright-green suit is really a hard shell of armor. So don't underestimate this Pokémon because it's adorable—that's its best disguise! Quilladin is one tough Pokémon to pin on the battlefield.

CHESNAUGHT
The Spiny Armor Pokémon

Height: 5' 03"
Weight: 198.4 lbs.
Type: Grass-Fighting

CHESPIN

QUILLADIN

CHESNAUGHT

The Spiny Armor Pokémon stands tall! Chesnaught is five times taller than its original form, Chespin. And that's not all! It's also ten times heavier—and it's evolved into a Fighting-type.

Chesnaught can use its size alone to shield its friends from attack. The tough armor shell on its back strengthens its impressive shape. Chesnaught's casing is powerful enough to protect it from a fiery explosion. And its spikes will prevent an opponent from jumping on its back to attack. It you want to tangle with Chesnaught, you have to fight it face-to-face!

FENNEKIN
The Fox Pokémon

Height: 1' 04"
Weight: 20.7 lbs.
Type: Fire

WARNING: If you try to pet Fennekin's fuzzy ears, you might get burned! The air that comes out of them can reach 400° Fahrenheit—that's hot enough to melt asphalt!

The Fox Pokémon has an appetite for battle and for wood. It fuels its fierce fur blaze by snacking on small twigs in the same way you'd feed a campfire with kindling. After it chomps down on wood chips, it's ready to fire up its powerful attacks.

Before Ash's pal Serena set foot in Professor Sycamore's lab, she knew Fennekin was the First Partner for her. Fennekin soon proved it was a true friend by protecting her from a wild Vespiquen. It used its fiery Ember attack to surround the Beehive Pokémon.

FENNEKIN

BRAIXEN

DELPHOX

BRAIXEN
The Fox Pokémon

Height: 3' 03"
Weight: 32.0 lbs.
Type: Fire

Braixen is a fierce Fire-type that can set a battlefield ablaze. When Braixen pulls the twig out of its tail, it's like striking a match. The stick rubs against its fur, igniting a fire that turns the kindling into a fiery torch.

At the first Pokémon Showcase Ash attended, he spotted Aria, the famous Pokémon Performer. Aria's Pokémon pal Fennekin evolved into Braixen right there in front of the crowd. Then Braixen showed off its amazing fire-breathing skills. While it danced, it blew at the blaze on its twig to create a beautiful swirl called the Fire Spin. Aria's Braixen really knows how to get an audience all fired up!

FENNEKIN

BRAIXEN

DELPHOX

DELPHOX
The Fox Pokémon

Height: 4' 11"
Weight: 86.0 lbs.
Type: Fire-Psychic

The final evolved form of Fennekin, Delphox has evolved both in strength and in wisdom. Now a Psychic-type as well as a Fire-type, Delphox has the powers of a fortune-teller. Delphox experiences mystical and powerful visions. When it focuses its mind on the flame at the tip of its torch, it can see the future. It can also channel its Psychic-type abilities to create a spiral of flames that burns so brightly, they become white-hot. So don't cross this Pokémon, or it just might backfire!

FENNEKIN

BRAIXEN

DELPHOX

FROAKIE
The Bubble Frog Pokémon

Height: 1' 00"
Weight: 15.4 lbs.
Type: Water

FROAKIE

FROGADIER

GRENINJA

Froakie has very sensitive skin, but it's even more sensitive to its surroundings. Its skin helps it sense changes to its environment.

That soft white stuff around Froakie's neck isn't a stylish scarf to protect it from the weather. It's actually a shield made entirely of bubbles! Unlike soap bubbles that pop with a poke, the gummy ones on Froakie's neck and back are strong enough to withstand attacks.

Those bubbles can also blast off Team Rocket! When Wobbuffet's Mirror Coat made it impossible to attack, Froakie used its foam to save the day. Ash was impressed by this Pokémon's brave and caring nature. Soon after, the Bubble Frog Pokémon friend joined Ash on his journey—officially becoming the first Pokémon Ash caught in Kalos.

FROGADIER

The Bubble Frog Pokémon

Height: 2' 00"
Weight: 24.0 lbs.
Type: Water

The Bubble Frog Pokémon is known for its incredible talent for jumping and climbing, but perhaps its most impressive skill is its aim. When it flings pebbles dipped in a coat of foamy bubbles, Frogadier can hit a target that's a hundred feet away!

It took the perfect challenger to evolve Ash's pal Froakie: a ninja. During a battle with a masked man, Froakie gathered all its strength. The Bubble Frog Pokémon wound up being so mighty, it evolved mid-battle. It finished the fight as Frogadier.

FROAKIE

FROGADIER

GRENINJA

GRENINJA
The Ninja Pokémon

Height: 4' 11"
Weight: 88.2 lbs.
Type: Water-Dark

FROAKIE

FROGADIER

GRENINJA

The Ninja Pokémon lives up to its name. The stealthy Water- and Dark-type likes to sneak up on its enemies. It travels in shadows, sliding in and out of sight. By the time you see Greninja, it's too late to prepare for its attack.

Greninja has sharp Moves and can make an even sharper weapon. It has enough might to press water so tightly between its hands that it can shape the liquid into a throwing star that can cut through metal. Water usually makes a splash, but with Greninja, water can also slash!

FLETCHLING

The Tiny Robin Pokémon

Height: 1' 00"
Weight: 3.7 lbs.
Type: Normal-Flying

FLETCHLING

FLETCHINDER

TALONFLAME

The little Normal- and Flying-type uses its lovely melodies to communicate with its entire flock. Each ditty is a signal. No matter what the word is, it's always music to a passerby's ears.

While the sounds coming from its beak are sweet, Fletchling's Big Pecks can turn an enemy into mincemeat. Fletchling is very protective of its place and pals. If you trample its territory, it will join forces with its flock and fight back.

Clemont tried to help Ash catch wild Fletchling with his Flying-type Pokémon Attractor Machine. But all it attracted was a swarm of angry Beedrill! Ash wouldn't give up on catching Fletchling, and fortunately, his Froakie was ready to help. Froakie leaped from cliff to cliff and was finally able to defeat the Normal- and Flying-type.

FLETCHINDER
The Ember Pokémon

Height: 2' 04"
Weight: 35.3 lbs.
Type: Fire-Flying

The Ember Pokémon really has fire in its belly! Its need for flying speed is ignited by the flame sac in its tummy. As it warms up, Fletchinder zooms through the sky.

Fletchinder's beak can fire embers that it uses to trick its prey. Fletchinder drops live coals on grassy fields to set them ablaze. When Pokémon pop up to see what's going on, Fletchinder pounces.

While visiting Kalos Canyon, Ash's pal Fletchling wanted a special match called a Sky Battle. Both Pokémon and their Trainers (wearing wing suits) battle in midair. But none of the other Flying-types thought Fletchling was worth their time . . . until it stopped a surprise attack from Team Rocket. When Talonflame finally agreed to battle it, Fletchling evolved into Fletchinder and won the match!

FLETCHLING

FLETCHINDER

TALONFLAME

TALONFLAME
The Scorching Pokémon

Height: 3' 11"
Weight: 54.0 lbs.
Type: Fire-Flying

The Scorching Pokémon can make it rain fire! As it flies through the skies, it can shower embers through the small openings in its feather coat. And that's not the only way it can heat up a battle! Talonflame can swoop in and attack with incredible speeds of up to 310 miles per hour. It's so fast, its foes better keep their eyes on the sky.

One thing's for sure: A battle with Talonflame is sure to be a heated match. And here's the real kicker—Talonflame likes to end a round by punting its prey!

FLETCHLING

FLETCHINDER

TALONFLAME

RIOLU

The Emanation Pokémon

Height: 2' 04"
Weight: 44.5 lbs.
Type: Fighting

RIOLU

LUCARIO

MEGA LUCARIO

No need to ask Riolu, "How are you?" The Emanation Pokémon is surrounded by colored light called an *aura*. The shape of the aura changes depending on Riolu's mood. You'll get the message it's trying to send by looking at that light. If you're bonded with Riolu, it can sense your aura, too.

Riolu communicates best on the battlefield. This Fighting-type Pokémon loves a good challenge. When Ash tried to rescue Riolu from evil Pokémon poacher Hunter J, he found a true kindred spirit. Their auras were a match, and Ash was able to send Riolu messages and secrets, no matter how far apart they were. Using this special communication, Ash was able to stop Hunter J and rescue Riolu.

LUCARIO
The Aura Pokémon

Height: 3' 11"
Weight: 119.0 lbs.
Type: Fighting-Steel

RIOLU

LUCARIO

MEGA LUCARIO

The evolved form of Riolu, Lucario is a Fighting-type and now a Steel-type, too. With all that toughness, you'd think its real power was its might. However, Lucario has an incredible strength that comes from an unexpected place—its understanding of unspoken emotion.

The Aura Pokémon is a sensitive soul. It is able to sense others' feelings deeply, and it can predict an opponent's next Move and even read someone's mind. Nothing gets past its keen insight! But it also has the battling power to back up its brains. Lucario is both a lover and a fighter.

MEGA LUCARIO
The Aura Pokémon

Height: 3' 11"
Weight: 119.0 lbs.
Type: Fighting-Steel

Amazingly enough, when Lucario becomes Mega Lucario, it grows even bigger and stronger. Mega Lucario's body is surging with aura energy. You can spot its impressive power in the black veins outlined on its body.

Ash helped fellow Trainer Korrina Mega-Evolve her Pokémon pal Lucario. For Lucario to evolve into Mega Lucario, it must have a deep bond of trust with its Trainer. So Korrina decided to win a hundred consecutive battles. As a reward for her hard work, Korrina's grandfather gave her a special Key Stone, the second piece of the puzzle. For the third and final piece, they visited Geosenge Town to find Lucarionite, a precious stone hidden deep in a cave. With all the pieces in place, Korrina and Lucario were able to finally realize their dream of Mega Evolution!

RIOLU

LUCARIO

MEGA LUCARIO

CARVANHA
The Savage Pokémon

Height: 2' 07"
Weight: 45.9 lbs.
Type: Water-Dark

This Water- and Dark-type is armed with sharp fangs and a tough jaw. When Carvanha opens wide, there's nowhere safe to hide! There's strength in numbers, and that's certainly Carvanha's motto. They like to stick together so they form an unstoppable chomping machine. A swarm of Carvanha can chew through and spit out pretty much anything they please, but the Savage Pokémon has a particular taste for boats. When they sink their teeth into a ship, it does just that—sinks!

Carvanha don't take kindly to intruders in their territory. If they spot anything or anyone in their watery quarters, these ferocious swimmers will band together and attack the intruder. So when you're traveling through the jungle, look out for the rivers Carvanha call home.

CARVANHA

SHARPEDO

MEGA SHARPEDO

SHARPEDO
The Brutal Pokémon

Height: 5' 11"
Weight: 195.8 lbs.
Type: Water-Dark

Sharpedo can slice through the water at 75 miles per hour—faster than the speed limit for cars on the highway. And this speedy swimmer doesn't have to worry about getting a ticket!

Sharpedo has impressive chompers it uses to catch foes. Known as "the Bully of the Sea," Sharpedo's reputation is as mean as its bite. Its fangs are so sharp, they can pierce through a sheet of steel. It can chew through a submarine like it's a peanut butter and jelly sandwich—and in no time, that big ship will be toast!

CARVANHA

SHARPEDO

MEGA SHARPEDO

MEGA SHARPEDO
The Brutal Pokémon

Height: 8' 02"
Weight: 287.3 lbs.
Type: Water-Dark

It's no easy task to befriend a bully, but it's especially tricky to warm up to one with this many sharp teeth! Trainers have to be both brave and patient to create the strong bond required to Mega-Evolve "the Bully of the Sea." Plus, Trainers must possess both a Key Stone and a special Mega Stone called Sharpedonite.

All that hard work is really worth it, though! In its Mega-Evolved form, Sharpedo grows roughly two feet longer and gains a hundred pounds. It also sprouts a row of sharp hornlike fangs on its nose. If one of those pointy prickles gets knocked out, a new one will instantly grow in. This Dark- and Water-type is always ready to sink its teeth into battle.

CARVANHA

SHARPEDO

MEGA SHARPEDO

BUNEARY
The Rabbit Pokémon

Height: 1' 04"
Weight: 12.1 lbs.
Type: Normal

With those big dark eyes and fluffy ears, itty-bitty Buneary looks adorable. But don't be fooled by its powers of cuteness. Inside is a real force of nature! The Rabbit Pokémon keeps its ears rolled up in soft poofs. Buneary keeps them in place to protect itself. When it unrolls those ears, they're powerful enough to bust through a boulder. That's a rock-solid defense!

Buneary depends on its ears for more than just battle. On chilly nights, Buneary burrows itself into its pillowy lobes to stay warm and cozy.

BUNEARY

LOPUNNY

MEGA LOPUNNY

LOPUNNY
The Rabbit Pokémon

Height: 3' 11"
Weight: 73.4 lbs.
Type: Normal

BUNEARY

LOPUNNY

MEGA LOPUNNY

This Normal-type Pokémon has a heightened sense of danger. It doesn't have a nose for news—it has its ears. When it picks up on a bad vibe, it hops into action!

Lopunny would rather run from danger than start a fight. It will flee the scene faster than you can say Lopunny. So unless its foe is willing to chase it, Lopunny will beat its opponent simply by winning the race.

If Lopunny does get caught in a fight, look out! Its battle style has a lot of kick. Its superstrong legs strike an opponent with quite a wallop.

MEGA LOPUNNY
The Rabbit Pokémon

Height: 4' 03"
Weight: 62.4 lbs.
Type: Normal-Fighting

To help Lopunny Mega-Evolve, a Trainer must earn its trust—which is no small task, since Lopunny is skittish. Its Trainer must possess patience—plus a Key Stone and a Mega Stone called Lopunite.

When Lopunny Mega-Evolves mid-battle, it instantly grows a few inches and loses ten pounds. But what it really gains is an advantage: The Normal-type Pokémon also becomes a Fighting-type. This makes the defensive Lopunny transform into a very offensive Mega Lopunny. In its Mega-Evolved form, it's ready to battle from its head to its toes! It swings its ears into action, and its legs get so strong, they'll kick-start any match.

BUNEARY

LOPUNNY

MEGA LOPUNNY

HONEDGE
The Sword Pokémon

Height: 2' 04"
Weight: 4.4 lbs.
Type: Steel-Ghost

There is truly a ghost inside this Steel- and Ghost-type Pokémon. Honedge is a sword that's inhabited by a departed spirit. So whatever you do, don't mistake this Pokémon for a sword and start swinging it around! Honedge doesn't even draw its blade to battle back an intruder. To get the best of the silly person who thinks it's a sword, it simply wraps its blue fringe around him and saps his energy. This mysterious ghost likes nothing more than to drain the life out of those foolish enough to think they can possess it. Honedge refuses to be a weapon for others.

HONEDGE

DOUBLADE

AEGISLASH

DOUBLADE
The Sword Pokémon

Height: 2' 07"
Weight: 9.9 lbs.
Type: Steel-Ghost

Have you ever heard the expression "two heads are better than one"? Well, in Doublade's case, two swords are better than one. The evolved form of Honedge, Doublade is an expert at wielding not just one blade, but two. The two blades are so in sync they act as one. They communicate through telepathy—they don't have to say a word; they just read each other's minds. This sixth sense gives Doublade power to slice and dice in a coordinated dance so intricate, they can shred their foes with ease. Even the most skilled swordsman won't be able to follow their talented twists!

HONEDGE

DOUBLADE

AEGISLASH

AEGISLASH
The Royal Sword Pokémon

Height: 5' 07"
Weight: 116.8 lbs.
Type: Steel-Ghost

HONEDGE

DOUBLADE

AEGISLASH

When Doublade evolves into one massive sword, it more than doubles in height and in form. Aegislash can come in both Blade and Shield Formes, but both possess a power that played an important role in history. According to legend, Aegislash was always by the side of history's greatest kings. Its service to these important leaders of the past earned it the name the Royal Sword Pokémon.

Aegislash played such a key role in the kings' courts because it has an incredibly useful strength— Spectral Power. When Aegislash utilizes this Spectral Power, it can control other people and Pokémon.

SCYTHER
The Mantis Pokémon

Height: 4' 11"
Weight: 123.5 lbs.
Type: Bug-Flying

SCYTHER

SCIZOR

MEGA SCIZOR

Speedy Scyther strikes hard and strikes fast. It's known for its quick reflexes, lightning-fast attacks, and sharp forearms. Thanks to its swift style, Scyther can surprise an opponent with its scythes—the crescent-shaped blades that make up its arms. The Bug- and Flying-type has another advantage, too: It can attack from land or swoop in from the sky.

If you get the chance to battle Scyther, stay on your toes and don't blink. Scyther can slash a foe before it even sees it coming. This combination of raw talent—speed and scythes—gives the Mantis Pokémon a real advantage over many of its enemies.

SCIZOR
The Pincer Pokémon

Height: 5' 11"
Weight: 260.91 lbs.
Type: Bug-Steel

SCYTHER

SCIZOR

MEGA SCIZOR

The evolved form of Scyther, Scizor trades in scythes for a pair of giant pincers. Its big red claws can catch a foe in its tight grip. Or, if it nabs an object, it can crush it simply by pinching. (Luckily, adults that like to pinch cheeks don't have Scizor's powerful squeeze!)

With pinching power like that, it's no wonder Scizor is called the Pincer Pokémon. But even before it uses its great grip, Scizor has markings to warn its enemies not to get too close. The yellow eyes on its claws are meant to confuse those who dare to challenge it.

MEGA SCIZOR
The Pincer Pokémon

Height: 6' 07"
Weight: 275.6 lbs.
Type: Bug-Steel

Trainers possessing a Key Stone can Mega-Evolve Scizor during battle with the aid of a special Mega Stone called Scizorite. In its Mega-Evolved form, its pinch gets even tougher. Mega Scizor's claws grow larger and are lined with sharp teeth. Now it has twice the bite!

Once Mega Scizor catches an opponent in its pincers, there's no escape. Its grip is so unbreakable and its pinch is so powerful that it can cut straight through concrete.

If you're brave enough to battle the Pincer Pokémon, avoid close combat. If your Pokémon is a Fairy-type, you have more than just its grasp to worry about—its Steel-type Moves will be extra effective against you in battle.

SCYTHER

SCIZOR

MEGA SCIZOR

SNOVER
The Frost Tree Pokémon

Height: 3' 03"
Weight: 111.3 lbs.
Type: Grass-Ice

Short and stout, Snover loves nothing more than hanging out on the mountains it calls home. With its white top and branchlike arms, it blends right into the snow-covered landscape. So you'll have to keep your eyes peeled to find one in the wild.

Here are a couple hints to help spot the Frost Tree Pokémon: During the winter, you'll find Snover romping around in the snow piles in the lower parts of the mountain. Once it turns to spring, Snover heads toward the peak. So if you're hoping to see these Grass- and Ice-types, you better bring your hiking boots!

SNOVER

ABOMASNOW

MEGA ABOMASNOW

ABOMASNOW
The Frost Tree Pokémon

Height: 7' 03"
Weight: 298.7 lbs.
Type: Grass-Ice

This frosty Pokémon is a real giant! It weighs nearly three hundred pounds (three times its previous form, Snover), making Abomasnow a physical powerhouse. It takes a lot to bring that big lug down!

Abomasnow's impressive shape combined with its misunderstood personality has earned it the nickname "the Ice Monster." But don't try to warm up to this distant Pokémon—it's a loner. Abomasnow has a cold personality that matches its love of wintry weather. To ensure it's left alone, the Grass- and Ice-type will create a blizzard to hide itself. If you pester this Pokémon, it'll live up to its nickname and you'll be caught in a crazy snowstorm.

SNOVER

ABOMASNOW

MEGA ABOMASNOW

MEGA ABOMASNOW
The Frost Tree Pokémon

Height: 8' 10"
Weight: 407.9 lbs.
Type: Grass-Ice

To make this magical Mega Evolution happen, a Trainer with a Key Stone must have its Abomasnow hold a precious crystal called Abomasite during battle. When Abomasnow Mega-Evolves, its height increases by over a foot and a half, making it over eight feet tall. It also gains more than a hundred pounds. Perhaps the biggest change is the two long ice shafts that sprout from its back.

Mega Abomasnow loves ice, snow, frost, and the cold so much that if another Pokémon tries to change the weather on the battlefield, Abomasnow will create a fierce hailstorm until it's winter again.

SNOVER

ABOMASNOW

MEGA ABOMASNOW

NOW YOU
SEE IT . . .

. . . NOW
YOU DON'T!